Zac Blasts Off
published in 2014 by
Hardie Grant Egmont
Ground Floor, Building 1, 658 Church Street
Richmond, Victoria 3121, Australia
www.hardiegrantegmont.com.au

A CiP record for this title is available from the National Library of Australia.

Text, design and illustration copyright © 2014 Hardie Grant Egmont

Illustrations by Tomomi Sarafov
Design by Stephanie Spartels
Zac Power logo design by Simon Swingler

Printed in China by WKT

1 3 5 7 9 10 8 6 4 2

ZAC BLASTS OFF

BY H.I. LARRY

ILLUSTRATIONS BY TOMOMI SARAFOV

hardie grant EGMONT

CHAPTER

Zac Power was about to ride

a new roller-coaster.

Everyone said it was fast and

scary. But Zac wasn't scared.

He liked fast things.

Zac was 12 years old. He was

a new Spy Recruit at GIB.

They were a spy group.

GIB sent spies on missions.

They also stopped the evil spy group BIG from doing bad things.

GIB spies had code names. Zac's code name was Agent Rock Star.

Sometimes GIB sent Zac to Spy Camp. He loved going there. GIB trained Zac to do lots of cool stuff at Spy Camp.

He learnt how to scuba-dive
and crack codes.

Zac was nearly at the start of
the line for the roller-coaster.
His SpyPad beeped.

Every GIB spy had a SpyPad.
It was a mini tablet. Zac liked
to put games and songs on his.

Zac looked at his SpyPad.
He had a message from GIB.

Get into the last car

on the roller-coaster.

You're going to Spy Camp.

Awesome, thought Zac.

He walked down to the last car

and got in. The safety harness

came down over his shoulders.

Zac held on tight as the

roller-coaster shot off. It went

up and down and around.

The cars ahead of Zac turned left. At the last second, Zac's car turned right. He was racing down a secret tunnel!

CHAPTER 2

Zac sped through the tunnel.

He wondered what he would

be doing at Spy Camp.

GIB spies trained all over the

world. Even under the sea!

Zac arrived at Spy Camp.
He got off the roller-coaster.

Spy Camp was a big silver
dome. There was a canteen
and a games room in the
middle. There were big doors
all around the edge.

All of GIB's training gear
was stored in rooms behind
the doors.

Hanging from the roof
was a huge TV screen.
It showed the latest Spy
Ladder results.

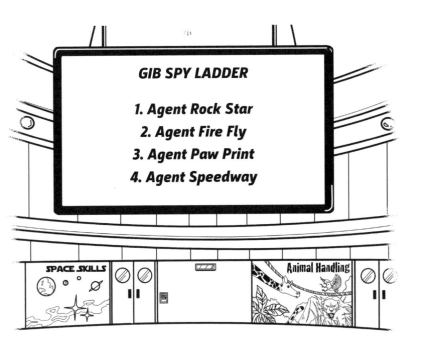

GIB spies got points for completing missions. They also got points for training at Spy Camp.

Zac had been on top of the Spy Ladder lots of times.

'Hello, Agent Rock Star,' said a spy at the front desk.

He handed Zac an Info-Disk. Info-Disks told spies what they would be doing at Spy Camp.

Zac put the Info-Disk into his SpyPad.

A message popped up.

Spy Camp Skill:
Space Skills

Training Buddy:
Agent Speedway

Training Place:
GIB Space Base

Cool! thought Zac. *Space skills with Agent Speedway will be fun.*

Zac had met Agent Speedway at a GIB sports day. His real name was Andy. He was the same age as Zac. Andy liked to win all the time. But Zac still liked him.

'Zac,' called Agent Speedway from across the dome.

'The Space Skills room is here!'

Zac went over to Agent Speedway.

'Hi, Andy,' said Zac.

Zac and Andy scanned their SpyPads over the door.

The door opened.

Everything that they needed for space travel was inside.

Andy and Zac put on their space suits. The suits were ultra-light. They had cool satellite radios built in.

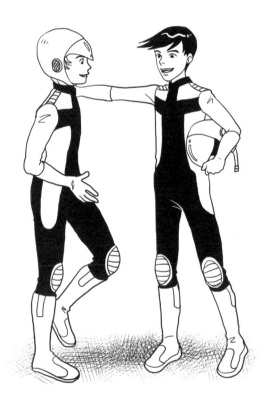

There were two mini space ships sitting on a launch pad in the room.

They looked like racing cars with turbo jets instead of wheels. They had 'Space Racer' printed on them.

Zac checked out his Space Racer. Inside was a computer screen and lots of buttons.

Zac saw something sitting
on the seat. It looked like a
baseball glove with silver mesh
on the inside.

He looked at its label.

SONIC MITT.

CATCH ENEMY LASERS,

THEN THROW THEM BACK!

Awesome, thought Zac.

That might be handy in space.

There was a roller door at the back of the Space Skills room. It led outside. Zac pressed a button to open it.

Zac hopped into his Space Racer and fired up the jets.

'I'll race you there, Zac,' said Andy, taking off from the launch pad. Zac followed him.

They shot outside.

WHOOOOOOSH!

As they got further into space everything outside got darker.

After a few hours they flew past the moon. It was covered with craters. They looked like elephant footprints.

Zac turned on the auto-pilot.

'Hey, Andy,' said Zac through

the radio. 'Want to play

Space Blast 4?'

'Totally,' said Andy.

Zac logged in and they played each other online.

They had to dodge laser blasts. On each level the blasts went faster. They played for ages. It was close but Zac was winning.

Suddenly, Zac's screen flashed.

You have reached the

GIB Space Base.

CHAPTER

Zac and Andy flew inside the
Space Base. There was a man
in a space suit waiting inside.

'My name is Agent Moon
Rock,' said the man.

Zac had heard of Agent Moon Rock. He was GIB's best space spy. He had lived in space for 30 years!

'Today you'll practise space skills,' said Agent Moon Rock. 'Then you'll be tested. I'll stay at the Space Base and talk to you through the radio. Let's get started!'

Zac and Andy flew out of the base in their Space Racers. Agent Moon Rock's voice came over the radio.

'Lots of things float around in space,' said Agent Moon Rock. 'They can be dangerous.'

'Like this!' said Zac. Some space junk was flying towards him.

FWOOSH!

Zac turned the Space Racer sharply and got out of the way.

'Exactly,' said Agent Moon Rock. 'Good job, Zac! GIB have set up a practice course. You need to fly through it and dodge the space junk.'

Zac and Andy flew through the course. Andy flew very fast. Soon Zac couldn't see him.

Zac saw an asteroid and

swerved quickly. Then a red

rocket came straight at him.

Zac dodged that, too.

Zac finished the practice course. Andy was waiting for him at the end.

'Come on, slow coach, it's test time,' said Andy over the radio.

Zac hated tests. But at least this test was in outer space!

CHAPTER

'This test is a race,' said Agent

Moon Rock through the

radio. 'GIB have set up space

objects along the course.

You have to dodge them.'

'Then you will get a score out of ten. The points will go on the Spy Ladder,' he added.

'See you at the finish line,' teased Andy. He zoomed away.

Zac followed Andy and they **ZIG-ZAGGED** through the course. Zac didn't want to lose his top spot on the Spy Ladder. He had to beat Andy!

Zac knew Andy was a fast driver. But Zac was very good at dodging space objects.

A meteor flew past Zac. He saw it and quickly moved out of the way. Zac's screen flashed.

Great driving!

Zac saw a piece of space junk coming towards them.
He ducked out of the way, but Andy was too late.

The junk scraped along Andy's Space Racer. Andy's Space Racer slowed down. Its fuel tank was leaking.

'Whoops,' said Andy. 'I'm OK! But I think my Space Racer needs fixing.'

'Stand by for a rescue ship, Andy,' said Agent Moon Rock. 'Zac, finish the course.'

Zac drove past Andy's Space

Racer. He was nearly at the

finish line.

Suddenly...

WHOOOSH!

Something raced past and fired a laser at Zac.

He swerved and only just got out of the way.

Zac looked out the window. There was a space ship with laser shooters on it.

Zac's computer screen flashed.

Danger! BIG Doom Striker

'Agent Moon Rock!' said Zac. 'There's a BIG Doom Striker on the course!'

'Return to the Space Base!' said Agent Moon Rock. 'Doom Strikers are remote-controlled and deadly.'

It was too late. The Doom Striker was heading straight for Zac!

CHAPTER 5

The Doom Striker fired more
lasers at Zac.

He dodged out of their way
quickly. He had to get back
to the Space Base.

Suddenly, the Doom Striker
turned away from Zac. It was
flying towards Andy.

Oh, no! thought Zac. *Andy's
Space Racer is broken. He can't
escape. I have to help him!*

Zac spun his Space Racer
around.

He flew towards Andy.

ZOOM!

He had to beat the Doom Striker.

Zac pulled out his Sonic Mitt from under the seat. He put it on. Then he raced his Space Racer in front of the Doom Striker.

'Are you crazy, Zac?!' yelled Andy through the radio.

'Don't worry,' said Zac. 'I have a plan.'

Zac opened the cockpit dome.

A laser came towards him.

PEOW!

He reached up and caught it

with the Sonic Mitt.

His hand tingled.

Zac threw the laser back as hard as he could.

The Doom Striker exploded.

It looked like shooting stars were flying everywhere.

Zac threw a rope over to Andy. 'Tie this to your Space Racer,' he said. 'I'll tow you back.'

CHAPTER

Zac landed in the Space Base.

'Well done, Zac,' said Agent Moon Rock.

'Yeah, thanks, Zac,' said Andy.

'You saved my life.'

Agent Moon Rock repaired
Andy's Space Racer. Then it
was time to go back to
Spy Camp.

'You'll find out the test results
there,' said Agent Moon Rock.

He waved goodbye as Zac and
Andy left the Space Base.
They flew back to Earth.

Andy flew very carefully.

Back at Spy Camp, Zac and

Andy went to the games room.

They finished playing Space

Blast 4.

Zac won. His Spy Camp practice had helped him. He could dodge the blasts really well.

Zac got a message on his SpyPad. It was his test results.

You have great vehicle control,

Agent Rock Star.

You are very brave, too.

10 points

'It was fun hanging out, Zac,' said Andy. 'We had a real blast.'

'Yeah,' said Zac. 'A space blast!'

The boys laughed.

Zac looked up at the Spy Ladder. It was being updated. Zac was still number one.

POWER

=SPY RECRUIT=

HAVE YOU READ THEM ALL?

WWW.ZACPOWER.COM